Astrid Mason

Princess Coloring Book for Kids

50 Amazing Facts and Cute Coloring Pages for Girls

Many princesses wear beautiful dresses and crowns, which are symbols of their royal status.

Princesses often live in magnificent castles with big towers, secret passages, and grand ballrooms.

Some princesses in fairy tales have magical powers, such as the ability to talk to animals or control the weather.

Princesses love to read books and learn new things. They are often very intelligent and curious.

Many princesses have animal
friends, such as birds, rabbits, or
even dragons!

Princesses enjoy dancing and attending grand balls. They learn to waltz and perform elegant dances.

Princesses can come from different parts of the world, such as Europe, Asia, Africa, and even imaginary lands!

Princesses often have special rooms in the castle, like a study filled with books, a music room with instruments, or a garden with beautiful flowers.

Princesses learn important skills like archery, horse riding, and fencing to protect themselves and their kingdom.

The term "American princess" is often used to describe influential women from wealthy and prominent families.

Some princesses have hidden talents, like playing musical instruments, painting, or storytelling.

Princesses have royal portraits
made, which capture their beauty
and grace.

Princesses have beautiful tiaras or crowns, which are usually passed down through generations.

Princesses sometimes have a
favorite magical creature, like a
unicorn or a mermaid.

Princesses often have a group of loyal knights who protect them and their kingdom.

Princesses have elegant and luxurious carriages, which they use for important events and royal processions.

Princesses sometimes have a fairy godmother who helps them in times of need.

Latin American princesses often participate in cultural celebrations, carnivals, and festivals, showcasing the rich traditions and folklore of their respective countries.

Princesses may have a special symbol or emblem that represents their family or kingdom.

Princesses often have a favorite
flower, like a rose, lily, or daisy.

Princesses have royal guards who protect the castle and ensure their safety.

Princesses may have special skills,
like playing chess, solving puzzles,
or riding a unicycle.

Princess Anastasia Romanov was the youngest daughter of Tsar Nicholas II, the last Russian emperor.

Princesses may have a magical key
that unlocks secret doors and
rooms in the castle.

African princesses may be skilled in traditional arts and crafts, such as pottery, weaving, or beadwork.

Princesses are skilled archers,
aiming their bows with precision
and hitting targets with impressive
accuracy.

Princesses have a unique connection with the stars and often gaze at the night sky, finding constellations and making wishes.

Princesses of Asia often wear beautiful traditional garments, such as saris, hanboks, kimonos, or cheongsams.

Future princesses will promote sustainable practices within their kingdoms, such as renewable energy sources and eco-friendly infrastructure.

Princess Diana, also known as the "People's Princess," captivated the world with her kindness and compassion.

Princesses have royal bedrooms adorned with elegant canopies, plush carpets, and exquisite furniture.

Future princesses will be proficient in coding and robotics, using their skills to create innovative solutions to societal problems.

Princess Sita, from the ancient Indian epic Ramayana, was known for her loyalty, bravery, and unwavering devotion to her husband.

Princesses have a royal library
filled with books from all over the
world.

Princess Kaiulani of Hawaii fought
tirelessly for Hawaiian
independence and became known
as the "Peacock Princess."

Princesses of the future will have robotic companions, capable of assisting them with various tasks and providing companionship.

Cleopatra, the last active ruler of ancient Egypt, was known as the "Princess of the Nile."

Future princesses will collaborate with scientists and researchers to develop innovative solutions for environmental challenges.

Princesses sometimes wear floral crowns made of colorful blossoms, adding a touch of natural beauty to their look.

Princesses have magical mirrors that can show them what's happening in different parts of the kingdom.

In ancient Greece, princesses like
Princess Helen of Troy were
famous for their beauty and played
a significant role in mythology.

Princesses have charming smiles
that can brighten up a room and
make everyone feel welcome.

Princesses often participate in
royal ceremonies, such as
coronations and royal weddings.

Some princesses have loyal animal
companions, such as talking horses,
wise owls, or mischievous cats.

African princesses are known for their vibrant and colorful traditional clothing and jewelry.

Princesses love to explore their kingdoms, discovering hidden treasures, and unraveling exciting mysteries.

Princesses enjoy outdoor picnics, where they indulge in delicious treats while basking in the warmth of the sun.

Asian princesses can be skilled in
martial arts, such as kung fu, judo,
or taekwondo.

Princesses are often skilled in sewing and embroidery and may create their own beautiful dresses.

Princesses may be patrons of museums and galleries, supporting the preservation and display of artwork and historical artifacts.